GRACE FOR GUS

HARRY BLISS

KT KATHERINE TEGEN BOOKS
An Imprint of HarperCollins Publishers

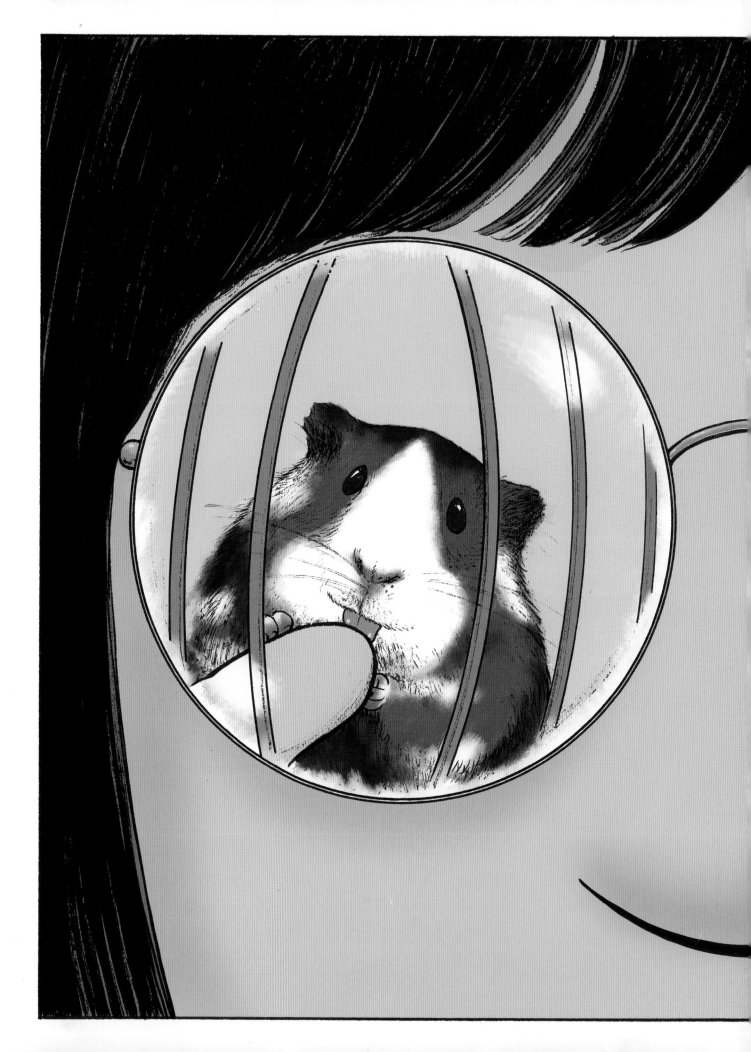

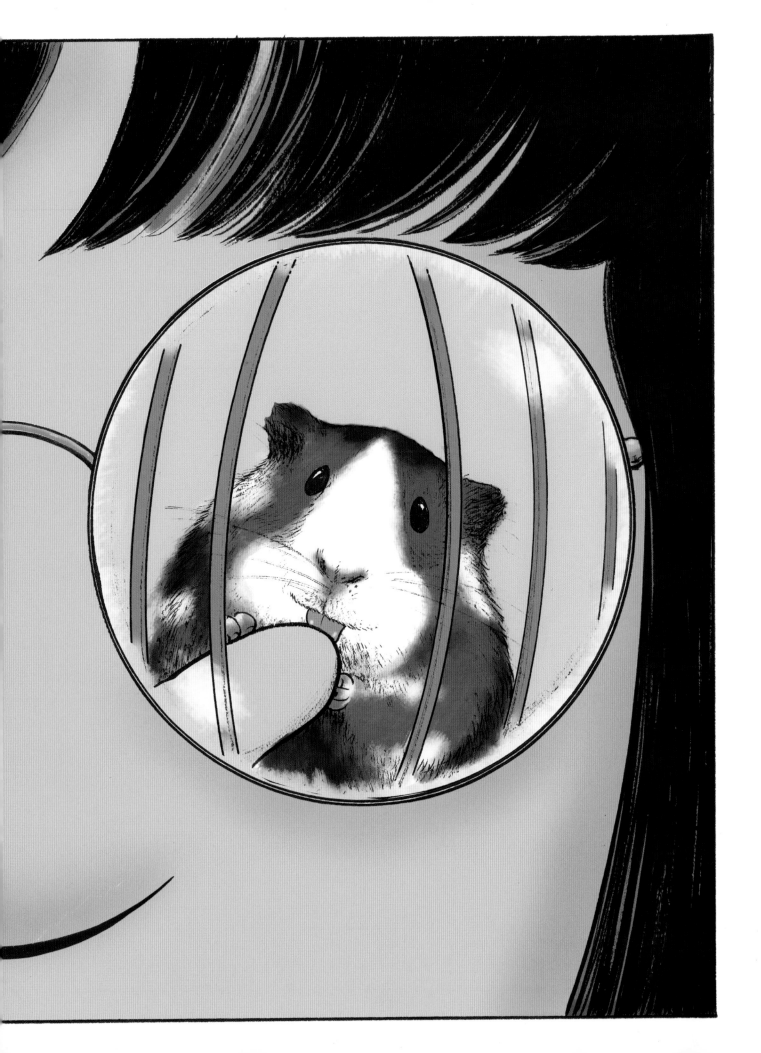

GRACE'S ROOM

BRAVO BRAVO

STREET

For my son and filmmaker,
Alexander Bliss, whose short film
this story is based on.

With thanks to colorist Frank Young

Katherine Tegen Books is an imprint of HarperCollins Publishers.

Grace for Gus
Copyright © 2018 by Harry Bliss
All rights reserved. Manufactured in China.
No part of this book may be used or reproduced in any manner whatsoever without
written permission except in the case of brief quotations embodied in critical articles
and reviews. For information address HarperCollins Children's Books, a division of
HarperCollins Publishers, 195 Broadway, New York, NY 10007.
www.harpercollinschildrens.com

Library of Congress Control Number: 2016963696
ISBN 978-0-06-264410-7

The artist used black India ink on Strathmore 2-ply paper to create the illustrations
for this book with color added digitally by Frank Young.

17 18 19 20 21 SCP 10 9 8 7 6 5 4 3 2 1
❖
First Edition